I Can Get It

and

Hop In!

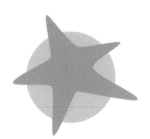

'I Can Get It' and 'Hop In!'
An original concept by Jenny Jinks
© Jenny Jinks

Illustrated by Louise Forshaw

Published by MAVERICK ARTS PUBLISHING LTD
Studio 3A, City Business Centre, 6 Brighton Road,
Horsham, West Sussex, RH13 5BB
© Maverick Arts Publishing Limited May 2018
+44 (0)1403 256941

A CIP catalogue record for this book is available at the British Library.

ISBN 978-1-84886-345-3

Maverick

www.maverickbooks.co.uk

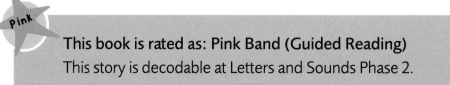

Pink

This book is rated as: Pink Band (Guided Reading)
This story is decodable at Letters and Sounds Phase 2.

I Can Get It

and

Hop In!

By
Jenny Jinks

Illustrated by
Louise Forshaw

The Letter C

Trace the lower and upper case letter with a finger. Sound out the letter.

Around

Around

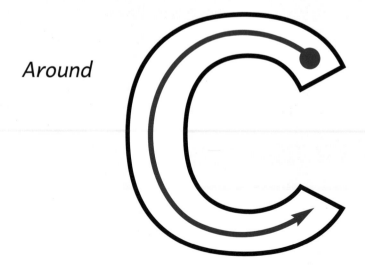

Some words to familiarise:

Mal   sad

High-frequency words:

is   I   it   oh   no

Tips for Reading 'I Can Get It'

- *Practise the words listed above before reading the story.*
- *If the reader struggles with any of the other words, ask them to look for sounds they know in the word. Encourage them to sound out the words and help them read the words if necessary.*
- *After reading the story, ask the reader why Mal is sad and how he gets his balloon back.*

Fun Activity

Discuss all the different ways to get Mal's balloon back.

I Can Get It

Mal is sad.

8

He cannot get it.

She cannot get it.

12

He cannot get it.

Mal is sad.

14

The Letter H

Trace the lower and upper case letter with a finger. Sound out the letter.

Down,
up,
around,
down

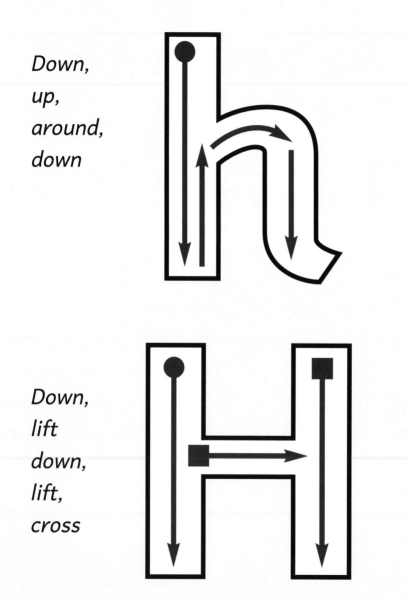

Down,
lift
down,
lift,
cross

Some words to familiarise:

Dan   car   bus

High-frequency words:

in is his I

Tips for Reading 'Hop In!'

- *Practise the words listed above before reading the story.*

- *If the reader struggles with any of the other words, ask them to look for sounds they know in the word. Encourage them to sound out the words and help them read the words if necessary.*

- *After reading the story, ask the reader what happens to Dan's car.*

Fun Activity

Discuss your favourite way to travel.

Hop In!

Dan is in his car.

Hop in!

25

Book Bands for Guided Reading

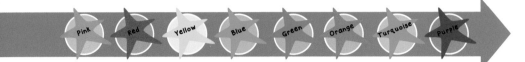

Book Band

Pink

978-1-84886-287-6 978-1-84886-286-9 978-1-84886-249-4 978-1-84886-285-2 978-1-84886-248-7

978-1-84886-346-0 978-1-84886-343-9 978-1-84886-345-3 978-1-84886-342-2 978-1-84886-344-6

Plus many more titles in the scheme!

To view the whole Maverick Readers scheme, please visit:

www.maverickbooks.co.uk/early-readers

The Institute of Education book banding system is a scale of colours that reflects the various levels of reading difficulty. The bands are assigned by taking into account the content, the language style, the layout and phonics.

Maverick Early Readers are a bright, attractive range of books covering the pink to purple bands. All of these books have been book banded for guided reading to the industry standard and edited by a leading educational consultant.